THIS LITTLE TIGER BOOK BELONGS TO:

Grace Fiona Swan

Love from Aunty Fee

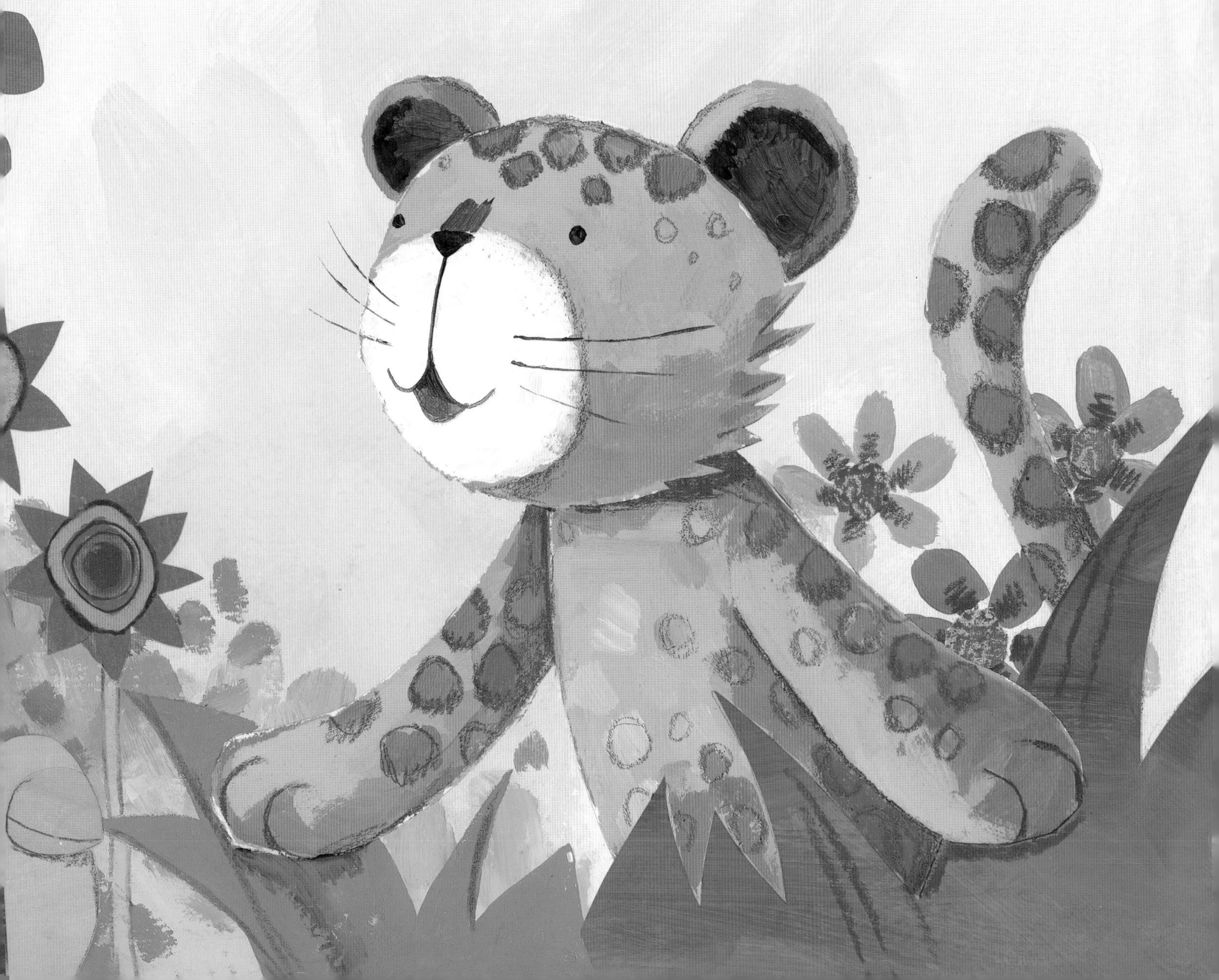

for the team at
Little Tiger Press
~ LJ

for Neil and Matthew
- JP

LITTLE TIGER PRESS
An imprint of Magi Publications
1 The Coda Centre, 189 Munster Road, London SW6 6AW
www.littletigerpress.com
First published in Great Britain 2001
This edition published 2002

Hide and Seek Birthday Treat

Linda Jennings and **Joanne Partis**

LITTLE TIGER PRESS
London

Leopard wakes up with a fluttery tummy.
"It's my birthday!" he shouts with great glee.
"I'm awfully excited, my friends are invited
to a yummy big birthday tea!"

Leopard eats breakfast, then leaves with a smile,
singing a bright birthday song.
He's going to bake a magnificent cake
for the friends he's inviting along.

Leopard calls first on his scruffy friend, Lion,
who lives in his smelly old den all alone.
There's no sound of roaring, or even of snoring.
Well Lion's not there – just a half-eaten bone!

Now Zebra lives out on the big windy plain.
Her stripes should be easy to see.
But there on the ground, not a hoofprint is found.
Could Zebra have gone on a spree?

Surely Tiger is back in his wild woody places,
after hunting all night 'neath the moon?
But a glance in his lair shows that Tiger's not there,
even though it is now nearly noon.

"Are you there, my friend Parrot?" calls Leopard.
"Don't you dare hide from me, silly bird!"
But everything's quiet where there's always a riot.
Not a squawk nor a screech can be heard.

Now Peacock would be a magnificent guest,
with his many-eyed tail on display.
He's loud and he's proud – he stands out in a crowd.
But where on earth is he today?

"Is Crocodile there in the water?
He's snappy and cunning and mean.
Perhaps he is basking – I'd rather not ask him."
Even Crocodile cannot be seen!

Poor Leopard begins to feel desperate.
"Perhaps I should ask Slippery Snake?
I can't hear him hissing, don't say he's gone missing.
Even he won't be sharing my cake!"

By teatime it's dark in the jungle,
and Leopard pads wearily home.
It's ever so sad, and really too bad
he must finish his birthday alone!

But when Leopard reaches his clearing,
a very strange sight meets his eyes!
A hundred small lights burn bright in the night.
Is this Leopard's birthday surprise?

Lion, Zebra and Tiger are waiting,
Parrot, Peacock and Crocodile too,
and even old Snake comes to share Leopard's cake,
and shout, "HAPPY BIRTHDAY TO YOU!"

More fantastic books from Little Tiger Press

For information regarding any of the above titles or for our full catalogue, please contact us:

Little Tiger Press, 1 The Coda Centre, 189 Munster Road, London SW6 6AW, UK

Tel: 020 7385 6333 Fax: 020 7385 7333 E-mail: info@littletiger.co.uk

www.littletigerpress.com

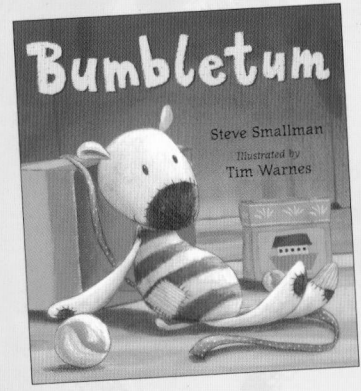

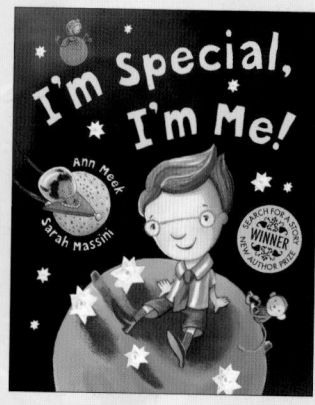

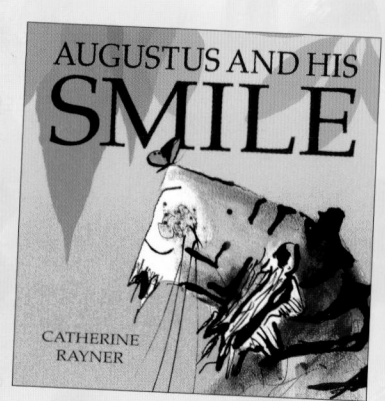

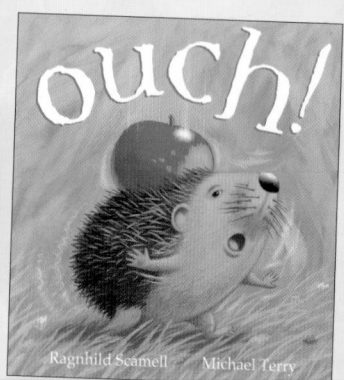

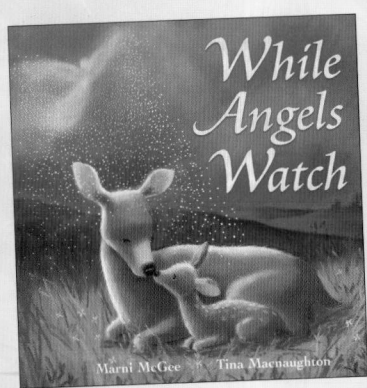

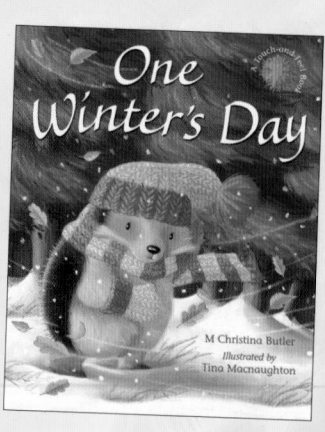

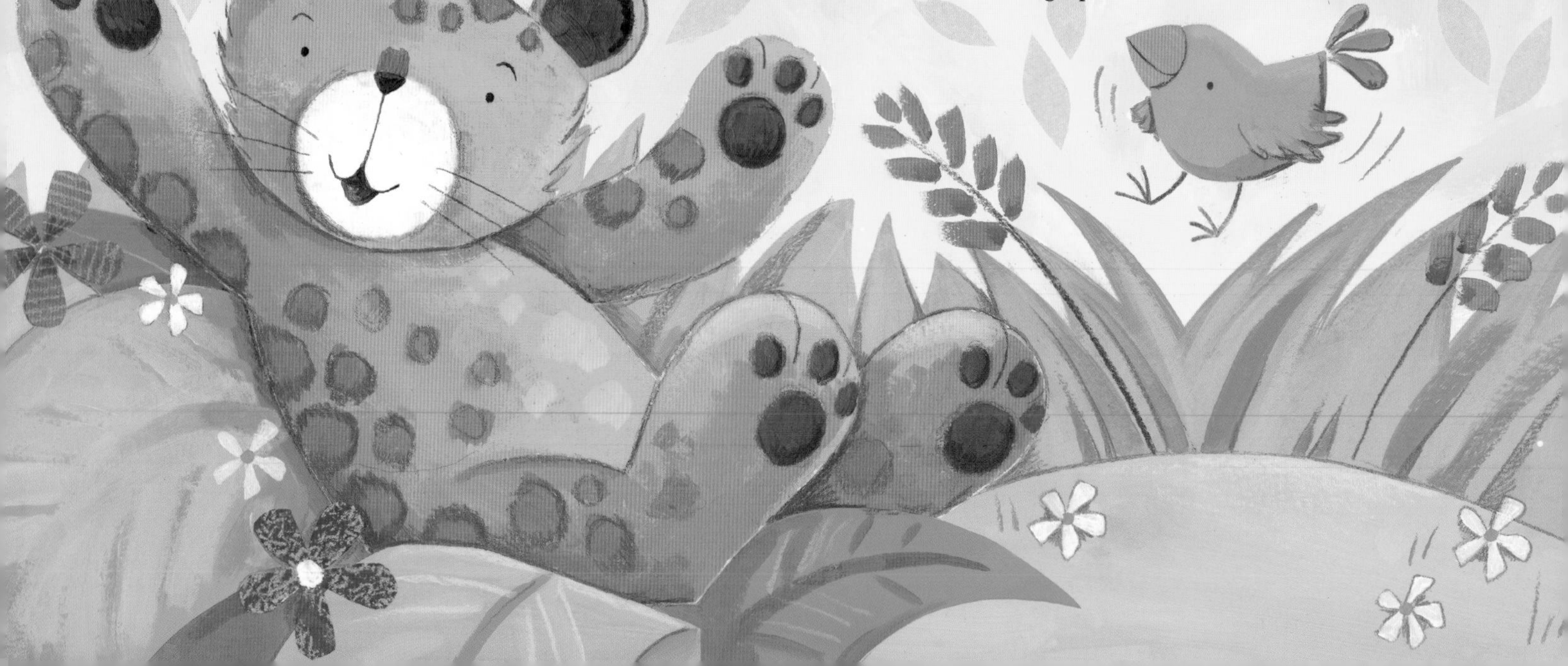